BE MISS

ARVIND

Copyright © Arvind
All Rights Reserved.

This book has been published with all efforts taken to make the material error-free after the consent of the author. However, the author and the publisher do not assume and hereby disclaim any liability to any party for any loss, damage, or disruption caused by errors or omissions, whether such errors or omissions result from negligence, accident, or any other cause.

While every effort has been made to avoid any mistake or omission, this publication is being sold on the condition and understanding that neither the author nor the publishers or printers would be liable in any manner to any person by reason of any mistake or omission in this publication or for any action taken or omitted to be taken or advice rendered or accepted on the basis of this work. For any defect in printing or binding the publishers will be liable only to replace the defective copy by another copy of this work then available.

be happy

Contents

Foreword   *vii*

Preface   *ix*

Acknowledgements   *xi*

Prologue   *xiii*

    1. India,   1

    2. After World   14

    3. Many Indian   17

Foreword

thanks

Preface

be happy

Acknowledgements

i am be

Prologue

good be

CHAPTER ONE

India,

India, officially the Republic of India (Hindi: Bhārat Gaṇarājya),[24] is a country in South Asia. It is the seventh-largest country by area, the second-most populous country, and the most populous democracy in the world. Bounded by the Indian Ocean on the south, the Arabian Sea on the southwest, and the Bay of Bengal on the southeast, it shares land borders with Pakistan to the west;[f] China, Nepal, and Bhutan to the north; and Bangladesh and Myanmar to the east. In the Indian Ocean, India is in the vicinity of Sri Lanka and the Maldives; its Andaman and Nicobar Islands share a maritime border with Thailand, Myanmar and Indonesia.

Modern humans arrived on the Indian subcontinent from Africa no later than 55,000 years ago.[25][26][27] Their long occupation, initially in varying forms of isolation as hunter-gatherers, has made the region highly diverse, second only to Africa in human genetic diversity.[28] Settled life emerged on the subcontinent in the western margins of the Indus river basin 9,000 years ago, evolving gradually into the Indus Valley Civilisation of the third millennium BCE.[29] By 1200 BCE, an archaic form of Sanskrit, an Indo-European language, had diffused into India from the northwest,[30][31] unfolding as the language of the Rigveda, and recording the dawning of Hinduism in India.[32] The Dravidian languages of India were supplanted in the northern and western regions.[33] By 400 BCE, stratification and exclusion by caste had emerged within Hinduism,[34] and Buddhism and Jainism had arisen, proclaiming social orders unlinked to heredity.[35] Early political consolidations gave rise to the loose-knit Maurya and Gupta Empires based in the Ganges Basin.[36] Their collective era was suffused with wide-ranging creativity,[37] but also marked by the declining status of women,[38] and the incorporation of untouchability into an organised system of belief.[g][39] In South India, the Middle kingdoms exported Dravidian-languages scripts and religious cultures to the kingdoms of Southeast Asia.[40]

In the early medieval era, Christianity, Islam, Judaism, and Zoroastrianism put down roots on India's southern and western coasts.[41] Muslim armies from Central Asia intermittently overran India's northern plains,[42] eventually establishing the Delhi Sultanate, and drawing northern India into the cosmopolitan networks of medieval Islam.[43] In the 15th century, the Vijayanagara Empire created a long-lasting composite Hindu culture in south India.[44] In the Punjab, Sikhism emerged, rejecting institutionalised religion.[45] The Mughal Empire, in 1526, ushered in two centuries of relative peace,[46] leaving a legacy of luminous architecture.[h][47] Gradually expanding rule of the British East India Company followed, turning India into a colonial economy, but also consolidating its sovereignty.[48] British Crown rule began in 1858. The rights promised to Indians were granted slowly,[49][50] but technological changes were introduced, and ideas of education, modernity and the public life took root.[51] A pioneering and influential nationalist movement emerged, which was noted for nonviolent resistance and became the major factor in ending British rule.[52] In 1947 the British Indian Empire was partitioned into two independent dominions, a Hindu-majority Dominion of India and a Muslim-majority Dominion of Pakistan, amid large-scale loss of life and an unprecedented migration.[53]

India has been a federal republic since 1950, governed in a democratic parliamentary system. It is a pluralistic, multilingual and multi-ethnic society. India's population grew from 361 million in 1951 to 1.211 billion in 2011.[54] During the same time, its nominal per capita income increased from US$64 annually to US$1,498, and its literacy rate from 16.6% to 74%. From being a comparatively destitute country in 1951,[55] India has become a fast-growing major economy and a hub for information technology services, with an expanding middle class.[56] It has a space programme which includes several planned or completed extraterrestrial missions. Indian movies, music, and spiritual teachings play an increasing role in global culture.[57] India has substantially reduced its rate of poverty, though at the cost of increasing economic inequality.[58] India is a nuclear-weapon state, which ranks high in military expenditure. It has disputes over Kashmir with its neighbours, Pakistan and China, unresolved since the mid-20th century.[59] Among the socio-economic challenges India faces are gender inequality, child malnutrition,[60] and rising levels of air pollution.[61] India's land is megadiverse, with four biodiversity hotspots.[62] Its forest cover comprises 21.7% of its area.[63] India's wildlife, which has traditionally been viewed with tolerance in India's culture,[64] is supported among these forests, and elsewhere, in protected habitats.

Contents

1 Etymology
2 History
2.1 Ancient India
2.2 Medieval India
2.3 Early modern India
2.4 Modern India
3 Geography
4 Biodiversity
5 Politics and government
5.1 Politics
5.2 Government
5.3 Administrative divisions
6 Foreign, economic and strategic relations
7 Economy
7.1 Industries
7.2 Energy
7.3 Socio-economic challenges
8 Demographics, languages, and religion
9 Culture
9.1 Visual art
9.2 Architecture
9.3 Literature
9.4 Performing arts and media
9.5 Society
9.6 Education
9.7 Clothing
9.8 Cuisine
9.9 Sports and recreation
10 See also
11 Notes

12 References
13 Bibliography
14 External links

Etymology

Main article: Names of India

According to the Oxford English Dictionary (third edition 2009), the name "India" is derived from the Classical Latin India, a reference to South Asia and an uncertain region to its east; and in turn derived successively from: Hellenistic Greek India (Ἰνδία); ancient Greek Indos (Ἰνδός); Old Persian Hindush, an eastern province of the Achaemenid empire; and ultimately its cognate, the Sanskrit Sindhu, or "river," specifically the Indus River and, by implication, its well-settled southern basin.[65][66] The ancient Greeks referred to the Indians as Indoi (Ἰνδοί), which translates as "The people of the Indus".[67]

The term Bharat (Bhārat; pronounced [ˈbʰaːrət] (listen)), mentioned in both Indian epic poetry and the Constitution of India,[68][69] is used in its variations by many Indian languages. A modern rendering of the historical name Bharatavarsha, which applied originally to North India,[70][71] Bharat gained increased currency from the mid-19th century as a native name for India.[68][72]

Hindustan ([ɦɪndʊˈstaːn] (listen)) is a Middle Persian name for India, introduced during the Mughal Empire and used widely since. Its meaning has varied, referring to a region encompassing present-day northern India and Pakistan or to India in its near entirety.[68][72][73]

History

Main articles: History of India and History of the Republic of India

Ancient India

An illustration from an early-modern manuscript of the Sanskrit epic Ramayana, composed in story-telling fashion c. 400 BCE – c. 300 CE.[74]

By 55,000 years ago, the first modern humans, or Homo sapiens, had arrived on the Indian subcontinent from Africa, where they had earlier evolved.[25][26][27] The earliest known modern human remains in South Asia date to about 30,000 years ago.[25] After 6500 BCE, evidence for domestication of food crops and animals, construction of permanent structures, and storage of agricultural surplus appeared in Mehrgarh and other sites in what is now Balochistan, Pakistan.[75] These gradually developed into the Indus Valley Civilisation,[76][75] the first urban culture in South Asia,[77] which flourished during 2500–1900 BCE in what is now Pakistan and western India.[78] Centred around cities such as Mohenjo-daro, Harappa, Dholavira, and Kalibangan, and relying on varied forms of subsistence, the civilisation engaged robustly in crafts production and wide-ranging trade.[77]

During the period 2000–500 BCE, many regions of the subcontinent transitioned from the Chalcolithic cultures to the Iron Age ones.[79] The Vedas, the oldest scriptures associated with Hinduism,[80] were composed during this period,[81] and historians have analysed these to posit a Vedic culture in the Punjab region and the upper Gangetic Plain.[79] Most historians also consider this period to have encompassed several waves of Indo-Aryan migration into the subcontinent from the north-west.[80] The caste system, which created a hierarchy of priests, warriors, and free peasants, but which excluded indigenous peoples by labelling their occupations impure, arose during this period.[82] On the Deccan Plateau, archaeological evidence from this period suggests the existence of a chiefdom stage of political organisation.[79] In South India, a progression to sedentary life is indicated by the large number of megalithic monuments dating from this period,[83] as well as by nearby traces of agriculture, irrigation tanks, and craft traditions.[83]

Cave 26 of the rock-cut Ajanta Caves

In the late Vedic period, around the 6th century BCE, the small states and chiefdoms of the Ganges Plain and the north-western regions had consolidated into 16 major oligarchies and monarchies that were known as the mahajanapadas.[84][85] The emerging urbanisation gave rise to non-Vedic religious movements, two of which became independent religions. Jainism came into prominence during the life of its exemplar, Mahavira.[86] Buddhism, based on the teachings of Gautama Buddha, attracted followers from all social classes excepting the middle class; chronicling the life of the Buddha was central to the beginnings of recorded history in India.[87][88][89] In an age of increasing urban wealth, both religions held up renunciation as an ideal,[90] and both established long-lasting monastic traditions. Politically, by the 3rd century BCE, the kingdom of Magadha had annexed or reduced other states to emerge as the Mauryan Empire.[91] The empire was once thought to have controlled most of the subcontinent except the far south, but its core regions are now thought to have been separated by large autonomous areas.[92][93] The Mauryan kings are known as much for their empire-building and determined management of public life as for Ashoka's renunciation of militarism and far-flung advocacy of the Buddhist dhamma.[94][95]

The Sangam literature of the Tamil language reveals that, between 200 BCE and 200 CE, the southern peninsula was ruled by the Cheras, the Cholas, and the Pandyas, dynasties that traded extensively with the Roman Empire and with West and South-East Asia.[96][97] In North India, Hinduism asserted patriarchal control within the family, leading to increased subordination of women.[98][91] By the 4th and 5th centuries, the Gupta Empire had created a complex system of administration and taxation in the greater Ganges Plain; this system became a model for later Indian kingdoms.[99][100] Under the Guptas, a renewed Hinduism based on devotion, rather than the management of ritual, began to assert itself.[101] This renewal was reflected in a flowering of sculpture and architecture, which found patrons among an urban elite.[100] Classical Sanskrit literature flowered as well, and Indian science, astronomy, medicine, and mathematics made significant advances.[100]

Medieval India

Brihadeshwara temple, Thanjavur, completed in 1010 CE

The Qutub Minar, 73 m (240 ft) tall, completed by the Sultan of Delhi, Iltutmish

The Indian early medieval age, from 600 to 1200 CE, is defined by regional kingdoms and cultural diversity.[102] When Harsha of Kannauj, who ruled much of the Indo-Gangetic Plain from 606 to 647 CE, attempted to expand southwards, he was defeated by the Chalukya ruler of the Deccan.[103] When his successor attempted to expand eastwards, he was defeated by the Pala king of Bengal.[103] When the Chalukyas attempted to expand southwards, they were defeated by the Pallavas from farther south, who in turn were opposed by the Pandyas and the Cholas from still farther south.[103] No ruler of this period was able to create an empire and consistently control lands much beyond their core region.[102] During this time, pastoral peoples, whose land had been cleared to make way for the growing agricultural economy, were accommodated within caste society, as were new non-traditional ruling classes.[104] The caste system consequently began to show regional differences.[104]

In the 6th and 7th centuries, the first devotional hymns were created in the Tamil language.[105] They were imitated all over India and led to both the resurgence of Hinduism and the development of all modern languages of the subcontinent.[105] Indian royalty, big and small, and the temples they patronised drew citizens in great numbers to the capital cities, which became economic hubs as well.[106] Temple towns of various sizes began to appear everywhere as India underwent another urbanisation.[106] By the 8th and 9th centuries, the effects were felt in South-East Asia, as South Indian culture and political systems were exported to lands that became part of modern-day Myanmar, Thailand, Laos, Cambodia, Vietnam, Philippines, Malaysia, and Java.[107] Indian merchants, scholars, and sometimes armies were involved in this transmission; South-East Asians took the initiative as well, with many sojourning in Indian seminaries and translating Buddhist and Hindu texts into their languages.[107]

After the 10th century, Muslim Central Asian nomadic clans, using swift-horse cavalry and raising vast armies united by ethnicity and religion, repeatedly overran South Asia's north-western plains, leading eventually to the establishment of the Islamic Delhi Sultanate in 1206.[108] The sultanate was to control much of North India and to make many forays into South India. Although at first disruptive for the Indian elites, the sultanate largely left its vast non-Muslim subject population to its own laws and customs.[109][110] By repeatedly repulsing Mongol raiders in the 13th century, the sultanate saved India from the devastation visited on West and Central Asia, setting the scene for centuries of migration of fleeing soldiers, learned men, mystics, traders, artists, and artisans from that region into the subcontinent, thereby creating a syncretic Indo-Islamic culture in the north.[111][112] The sultanate's raiding and weakening of the regional kingdoms of South India paved the way for the indigenous Vijayanagara Empire.[113] Embracing a strong Shaivite tradition and building upon the military technology of the sultanate, the empire came to control much of peninsular India,[114] and was to influence South Indian society for long afterwards.[113]

Early modern India

In the early 16th century, northern India, then under mainly Muslim rulers,[115] fell again to the superior mobility and firepower of a new generation of Central Asian warriors.[116] The resulting Mughal Empire did not stamp out the local societies it came to rule. Instead, it balanced and pacified them through new administrative practices[117][118] and diverse and inclusive ruling elites,[119] leading to more systematic, centralised, and uniform rule.[120] Eschewing tribal bonds and Islamic identity, especially under Akbar, the Mughals united their far-flung realms through loyalty, expressed through a Persianised culture, to an emperor who had near-divine status.[119] The Mughal state's economic policies, deriving most revenues from agriculture[121] and mandating that taxes be paid in the well-regulated silver currency,[122] caused peasants and artisans to enter larger markets.[120] The relative peace maintained by the empire during much of the 17th century was a factor in India's economic expansion,[120] resulting in greater patronage of painting, literary forms, textiles, and architecture.[123] Newly coherent social groups in northern and western India, such as the Marathas, the Rajputs, and the Sikhs, gained military and governing ambitions during Mughal rule, which, through collaboration or adversity, gave them both recognition and military experience.[124] Expanding commerce during Mughal rule gave rise to new Indian commercial and political elites along the coasts of southern and eastern India.[124] As the empire disintegrated, many among these elites were able to seek and control their own affairs.[125]

A distant view of the Taj Mahal from the Agra Fort

A two mohur Company gold coin, issued in 1835, the obverse inscribed "William IV, King"

By the early 18th century, with the lines between commercial and political dominance being increasingly blurred, a number of European trading companies, including the English East India Company, had established coastal outposts.[126][127] The East India Company's control of the seas, greater resources, and more advanced military training and technology led it to increasingly assert its military strength and caused it to become attractive to a portion of the Indian elite; these factors were crucial in allowing the company to gain control over the Bengal region by 1765 and sideline the other European companies.[128][126][129][130] Its further access to the riches of Bengal and the subsequent increased strength and size of its army enabled it to annexe or subdue most of India by the 1820s.[131] India was then no longer exporting manufactured goods as it long had, but was instead supplying the British Empire with raw materials. Many historians consider this to be the onset of India's colonial period.[126] By this time, with its economic power severely curtailed by the British parliament and having effectively been made an arm of British administration, the company began more consciously to enter non-economic arenas like education, social reform, and culture.[132]

Modern India

Main article: History of the Republic of India

Historians consider India's modern age to have begun sometime between 1848 and 1885. The appointment in 1848 of Lord Dalhousie as Governor General of the East India Company set the stage for changes essential to a modern state. These included the consolidation and demarcation of sovereignty, the surveillance of the population, and the education of citizens. Technological changes—among them, railways, canals, and the telegraph—were introduced not long after their introduction in Europe.[133][134][135][136] However, disaffection with the company also grew during this time and set off the Indian Rebellion of 1857. Fed by diverse resentments and perceptions, including invasive British-style social reforms, harsh land taxes, and summary treatment of some rich landowners and princes, the rebellion rocked many regions of northern and central India and shook the foundations of Company rule.[137][138] Although the rebellion was suppressed by 1858, it led to the dissolution of the East India Company and the direct administration of India by the British government. Proclaiming a unitary state and a gradual but limited British-style parliamentary system, the new rulers also protected princes and landed gentry as a feudal safeguard against future unrest.[139][140] In the decades following, public life gradually emerged all over India, leading eventually to the founding of the Indian National Congress in 1885.[141][142][143][144]

The rush of technology and the commercialisation of agriculture in the second half of the 19th century was marked by economic setbacks and many small farmers became dependent on the whims of far-away markets.[145] There was an increase in the number of large-scale famines,[146] and, despite the risks of infrastructure development borne by Indian taxpayers, little industrial employment was generated for Indians.[147] There were also salutary effects: commercial cropping, especially in the newly canalled Punjab, led to increased food production for internal consumption.[148] The railway network provided critical famine relief,[149] notably reduced the cost of moving goods,[149] and helped

CHAPTER TWO

After World

After World War I, in which approximately one million Indians served,[150] a new period began. It was marked by British reforms but also repressive legislation, by more strident Indian calls for self-rule, and by the beginnings of a nonviolent movement of non-co-operation, of which Mohandas Karamchand Gandhi would become the leader and enduring symbol.[151] During the 1930s, slow legislative reform was enacted by the British; the Indian National Congress won victories in the resulting elections.[152] The next decade was beset with crises: Indian participation in World War II, the Congress's final push for non-co-operation, and an upsurge of Muslim nationalism. All were capped by the advent of independence in 1947, but tempered by the partition of India into two states: India and Pakistan.[153]

Vital to India's self-image as an independent nation was its constitution, completed in 1950, which put in place a secular and democratic republic.[154] It has remained a democracy with civil liberties, an active Supreme Court, and a largely independent press.[155] Economic liberalisation, which began in the 1990s, has created a large urban middle class, transformed India into one of the world's fastest-growing economies,[156] and increased its geopolitical clout. Indian movies, music, and spiritual teachings play an increasing role in global culture.[155] Yet, India is also shaped by seemingly unyielding poverty, both rural and urban;[155] by religious and caste-related violence;[157] by Maoist-inspired Naxalite insurgencies;[158] and by separatism in Jammu and Kashmir and in Northeast India.[159] It has unresolved territorial disputes with China[160] and with Pakistan.[160] India's sustained democratic freedoms are unique among the world's newer nations; however, in spite of its recent economic successes, freedom from want for its disadvantaged population remains a goal yet to be achieved.[161]

Geography

Main article: Geography of India

India accounts for the bulk of the Indian subcontinent, lying atop the Indian tectonic plate, a part of the Indo-Australian Plate.[162] India's defining geological processes began 75 million years ago when the Indian Plate, then part of the southern supercontinent Gondwana, began a north-eastward drift caused by seafloor spreading to its south-west, and later, south and south-east.[162] Simultaneously, the vast Tethyan oceanic crust, to its northeast, began to subduct under the Eurasian Plate.[162] These dual processes, driven by convection in the Earth's mantle, both created the Indian Ocean and caused the Indian continental crust eventually to under-thrust Eurasia and to uplift the Himalayas.[162] Immediately south of the emerging Himalayas, plate movement created a vast trough that rapidly filled with river-borne sediment[163] and now constitutes the Indo-Gangetic Plain.[164] Cut off from the plain by the ancient Aravalli Range lies the Thar Desert.[165]

The Tungabhadra, with rocky outcrops, flows into the peninsular Krishna river.[166]

Fishing boats lashed together before a monsoon storm in a tidal creek in Anjarle village, Maharashtra.

The original Indian Plate survives as peninsular India, the oldest and geologically most stable part of India. It extends as far north as the Satpura and Vindhya ranges in central India. These parallel chains run from the Arabian Sea coast in Gujarat in the west to the coal-rich Chota Nagpur Plateau in Jharkhand in the east.[167] To the south, the remaining peninsular landmass, the Deccan Plateau, is flanked on the west and east by coastal ranges known as the Western and Eastern Ghats;[168] the plateau contains the country's oldest rock formations, some over one billion years old. Constituted in such fashion, India lies to the north of the equator between 6° 44′ and 35° 30′ north latitude[i] and 68° 7′ and 97° 25′ east longitude.[169]

Many Indian

Many Indian species have descended from those of Gondwana, the southern supercontinent from which India separated more than 100 million years ago.[198] India's subsequent collision with Eurasia set off a mass exchange of species. However, volcanism and climatic changes later caused the extinction of many endemic Indian forms.[199] Still later, mammals entered India from Asia through two zoogeographical passes flanking the Himalayas.[192] This had the effect of lowering endemism among India's mammals, which stands at 12.6%, contrasting with 45.8% among reptiles and 55.8% among amphibians.[187]} Notable endemics are the vulnerable[200] hooded leaf monkey[201] and the threatened[202] Beddom's toad[202][203] of the Western Ghats.

A Chital (Axis axis) stag attempts to browse in the Nagarhole National Park in a region covered by a moderately dense[k] forest.[192]

India contains 172 IUCN-designated threatened animal species, or 2.9% of endangered forms.[204] These include the endangered Bengal tiger and the Ganges river dolphin. Critically endangered species include: the gharial, a crocodilian; the great Indian bustard; and the Indian white-rumped vulture, which has become nearly extinct by having ingested the carrion of diclofenac-treated cattle.[205] The pervasive and ecologically devastating human encroachment of recent decades has critically endangered Indian wildlife. In response, the system of national parks and protected areas, first established in 1935, was expanded substantially. In 1972, India enacted the Wildlife Protection Act[206] and Project Tiger to safeguard crucial wilderness; the Forest Conservation Act was enacted in 1980 and amendments added in 1988.[207] India hosts more than five hundred wildlife sanctuaries and thirteen biosphere reserves,[208] four of which are part of the World Network of Biosphere Reserves; twenty-five wetlands are registered under the Ramsar Convention.[209]

Politics and government